WHEN I GROW UP, I WANT TO PLAY FOR
PURDUE

Terry Hutchens

Illustrated by Phil Velikan

Watercolor llustration ©2018 Anna Timke

The names in this book are in honor of Gavin and Gwyn Miller from San Diego, California, who are the author's great-nephew and great-niece. They have probably never heard of Purdue but who knows maybe they'll grow up to one day play there or simply go to school there!

This book is dedicated to boys and girls of all ages who grow up wanting to one day play athletics at Purdue.

"Hey Gavin, have I ever told you that you're the best big brother in the whole wide world?"

"Ahhh thanks Gwyn. You're a really good sister, too."

"Hey Gavin, do you ever think about what you want to be when you grow up?"

"Yeah, Gwyn, I think about it all the time."

"Or I bet you would be a good doctor, too."

"Or maybe a police officer. Then you could catch all the bad guys."

"Or maybe a teacher. Wouldn't you like to grow up to be like your fourth grade teacher, Mr. Johnson?"

"I wish I could play basketball at Purdue."

"I want to play basketball at Purdue, too."

"But I really love baseball. I could see myself playing baseball at Purdue."

"I could play softball at Purdue. That would be really cool."

"Or maybe I could wrestle at Purdue. That would be fun."

"I could play soccer at Purdue. I would be a good goalie."

"There are so many sports I could see myself playing. I really like to swim so maybe I could be on the swim team. Or dad showed me how to play tennis. Maybe I could do that."

"I know what you mean. There are so many different sports. I could see myself swimming or maybe hitting that tennis racket, too."

"Or maybe I could play football at Purdue. I could see myself playing quarterback or maybe running the football."

"Do you think I could play football at Purdue, Gavin? Maybe I could be the kicker."

"I don't know why not Gwyn. I think you can be whatever you want to be."

"I just think it would be really fun to be in the Purdue uniform and wear black and gold. And be a Boilermaker."

"Do you think that's something we could do together, Gavin?"

"I don't know why not, Gwyn."

"And you know what? Even if we don't grow up to play sports at Purdue, I think it would be fun if we both went to school there."